For Sophie and Papa John, with endless love xx

WORTHY Kids™

ISBN: 978-1-5460-0221-5

WorthyKids
Hachette Book Group
1290 Avenue of the Americas
New York, NY 10104

First published in Great Britain in 2022 by Hodder and Stoughton under the title *Tiny Blue, I Love You*

WorthyKids is a registered trademark of Hachette Book Group, Inc.

Library of Congress Cataloging-in-Publication Data

Names: Empson, Jo, author, illustrator.
Title: Papa loves you, Tiny Blue / written and illustrated by Jo Empson.
Description: New York, NY : WorthyKids, [2022] | Audience: Ages 3-6. |
  Summary: As they explore their watery world together, Papa patiently
  answers all of Tiny Blue's questions, including the biggest question of
  all: what is love?
Identifiers: LCCN 2021046234 | ISBN 9781546002215 (hardcover)
Subjects: CYAC: Questions and answers—Fiction. | Fathers and
  sons—Fiction. | Curiosity—Fiction. | Little blue penguin—Fiction. |
  Penguins—Fiction. | LCGFT: Picture books.
Classification: LCC PZ7.1.E48 Pap 2022 | DDC [E]—dc23
LC record available at https://lccn.loc.gov/2021046234

Printed and bound in China • APS
10 9 8 7 6 5 4 3 2 1

Papa
Loves You,
Tiny Blue

Written and illustrated by JO EMPSON

Tiny Blue was very little, but his head was filled
with very **BIG** questions.

He thought his papa was very wise. He must know
the answers to EVERYTHING.

"How old is the ocean?" Tiny Blue asked his papa.

"It's older than you
or me, Tiny Blue," said Papa.
"It's even older than our great-
great-great-great-great
grandparents."

Wow! That's very old, thought Tiny Blue.

He peered into the water.
A tiny blue penguin with big feet
and little wings looked back at him.

"Papa?"
he asked . . .

"why can't I fly?
Will I learn some day?"

Papa smiled. "Penguins aren't born to fly, Tiny Blue. Our wings are too small.

"But we were born to . . .

"SWIM!"

WOOHOOOOOOOOOOOOOOOOOOoo!

"So that's why I have such big feet!" cried Tiny Blue.

"Papa?"

"Yes, Tiny Blue?"

"What are those
wibbly wobbly
things?"

Above their heads,
hundreds of creatures
bobbed and swayed,
lighting up the ocean like
colorful fairy lights.

"They're **jellyfish**,
Tiny Blue."

"**Wow!**" gasped
Tiny Blue.

Now Tiny Blue and Papa plunged deep, deep down, toward the sleeping coral and swaying seagrass. All around them were creatures of every size and color. Tiny Blue was full of curiosity.

"Papa?"

"Yes, Tiny Blue?"

"What is the **biggest** fish in the ocean?"

"Is it true that daddy seahorses have babies?"

"the whale shark—look!"

"It's very big and scary," gasped Tiny Blue.

"It may be very big, but whale sharks are gentle giants," said Papa.

"But these seals aren't
as friendly as they look.
They like to eat penguins for lunch!

"Quick, swim as fast as you
can, Tiny Blue! And no
more questions!"

"Papa?"

"Yes, Tiny Blue?"

"Will you always keep me safe?"

"I will always keep you safe, Tiny Blue,"
said Papa. "There's no question about that."

As the sun set, Tiny Blue and his papa
swam to the shore.

"Papa?" asked Tiny Blue.
"How do you always know the way home?"

"I follow the same path every time, Tiny Blue.
One day I will teach you, and then you will know it forever."

"How long is forever, Papa?" asked Tiny Blue.

Papa smiled. "Aren't you tired yet?"

Tiny Blue and his papa settled down in their nest in the soft sand.

"Papa, do you know the answer to everything?"

"Nobody in the world knows the answer to everything," said Papa.
"Some questions are so big we will never know the answer.

"Now, good night, Tiny Blue. I love you."

"Papa?"

"Yes, Tiny Blue?"

"What is love?"

"Oh, Tiny Blue, that's a VERY big question.
It's one of life's greatest mysteries."

"But if it's a mystery," whispered Tiny Blue,
"then how do you know you love me?"

Tiny Blue's papa cuddled
him tight.

"I just do, Tiny Blue . . .

"I just do."

Tiny Blue is a little penguin. Little penguins are also known as fairy penguins or blue penguins and are the smallest penguins in the world. They like to live in warm places, such as Australia or New Zealand.

HERE ARE THE ANSWERS TO SOME OF TINY BLUE'S QUESTIONS:

"Is it true that daddy seahorses have babies?"
Yes, absolutely true. The seahorse daddy carries his babies in a pouch, just like a kangaroo.

"Do starfish live in the sky as well as the sea?"
No, the stars in the sky are very different. They are bundles of energy that glow and twinkle, and you can even wish upon them.

"Is there sand on the moon?"
There is something similar, but not quite like the sand we know. It's called *moon dust*.

Can you think of any other questions to ask Papa?